The Snapdragon was up to his tricks again. Every Tuesday he would whizz in and do nasty things to the words in the book.

His latest naughtiness was gobbling all the dots from the 'i's and blowing them at passers-by.

Phoot!

Phoot!

Phoot!

First published in 2009
by Hodder Children's Books.
This edition published in 2010.

Text and illustrations copyright © Mick Inkpen 2009

Hodder Children's Books
338 Euston Road, London, NW1 3BH

Hodder Children's Books Australia
Level 17/207 Kent Street, Sydney, NSW 2000

A catalogue record of this book is
available from the British Library.

ISBN: 978 0 340 98963 0
10 9 8 7 6 5 4 3

Printed in China

Hodder Children's Books is a
division of Hachette Children's Books.
An Hachette UK Company
www.hachette.co.uk

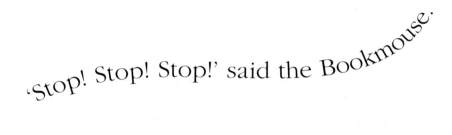

'Stop! Stop! Stop!' said the Bookmouse.

This is my Book!

Mick Inkpen

Hodder
Children's
Books

A division of Hachette Children's Books

But before anyone could
stop him, the Snapdragon
swooped down, bit off the k,
and part of the B of Book.

This is my Poo !

It was a **very** naughty thing to do.

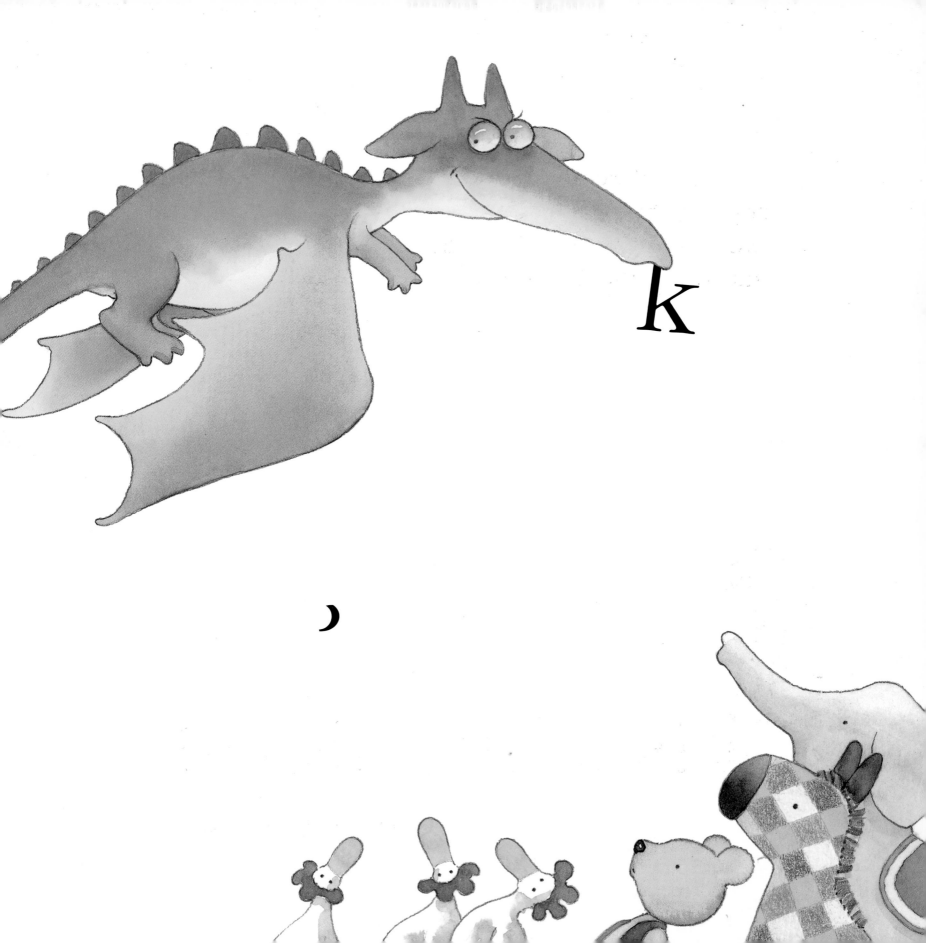

'You've got to do
something,' said the
Clockwork Penguin.
'He's getting worse!'
    The Bookmouse set
the missing part of the B
back in place and looked
at the new word.
    'Don't worry,' he said.
'I have a plan. What I
need is lots of those.'
    He was pointing
at the 'O's.

Boo

'I know where you can get 'O's,' said the Blink Owl mysteriously.

'You can get them where the ghosts of the Woollywolves l

But you'll have to be very brav

Look for the moon over the Moonwood.

Twit Twooo Twit Twooo Twit TWOOO

the middle of the Moonwood.

nd you'll have to hurry. It's happening soon, very soon.

Twit TWOOOOOOOOOOO

'You've got plenty of 'O's,'
said the Blue Bear. 'Can we have
some of those?'
But the Blink Owl had flown away.

That night under a low
moon they crept into the
Moonwood and waited.
     And before long, just as
the Blink Owl had said,
the 'O's began to arrive.
     'Ooooo,' they went,
whispering quietly through
the trees.

OOOOOOO

The 'O's grew louder.

And then louder still, wailing and howling through the trees.

OOOOO! OOOOOOOOOOOOO! OOOOOO OO

OOOO! OOOOOOO! OOOOO

'We don't like this,'
said the Little Horse.
And everyone
galloped out of the
Moonwood, leaving the
Bookmouse all alone.

The Bookmouse crept
further into the wood.
    'You don't frighten me!' he cried.
'Is that the best you can do?'
The Moonwood fell silent.
And then suddenly, louder than
any sound that had ever been heard
in the Moonwood before, there
came the most awful, rumbling…

OO

Quick as a flash, the
Bookmouse grabbed all the 'O's
and ran as fast as he could out
of the Moonwood.

'Give us back our 'O's!' cried
the ghosts of the Woollywolves.

And because he was a
very considerate mouse, the
Bookmouse tossed the smallest
one back to them.

said the ghosts of
the Woollywolves.

(It was all they *could* say.)

On Tuesday the Bookmouse set everyone in their places and went off to find the Snapdragon.

He was having his t

'Now this is your last
warning, Snapdragon!' said the
Bookmouse. 'The words don't
make any sense if you keep
eating the letters!
It's got to…

STOP.'

The Snapdragon
bit a chunk out of the 'P'.
   'I always eat my 'P's,'
he giggled.

Then he rose high into the air, sucking up all the little dots over the 'i's and blowing them straight at the Bookmouse.

Phoot!

Phoot!

Phoot!

'You can't tell me what to do!'

The Bookmouse scampered away as fast as he could with the Snapdragon snapping a

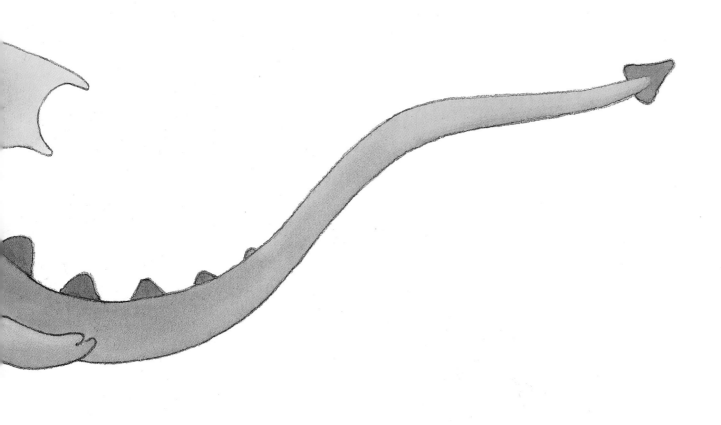

...le pink tail. As soon as he reached the edge of the page he squeaked loudly. Squeak! Squeak! Squeak!

And when they heard
the Bookmouse squeak,
everyone who lived at the
edge of the Moonwood took
a deep breath and shouted…

(And perhaps it would help if you joined in too.)

BOOOOC

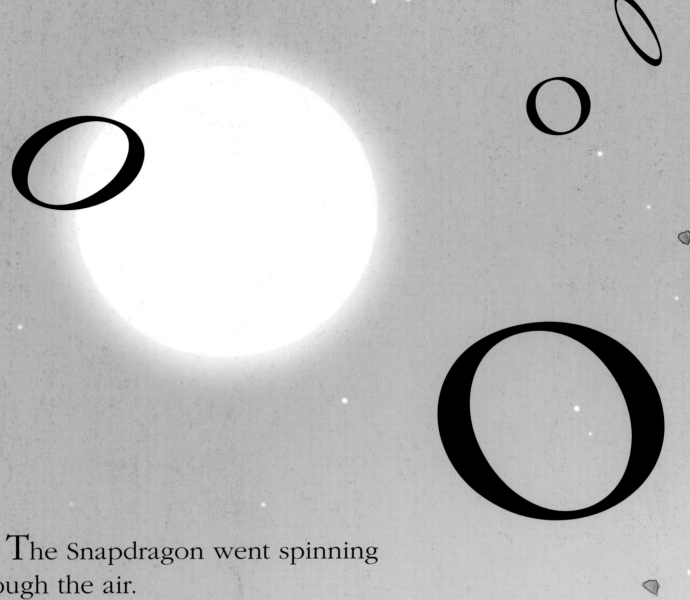

The Snapdragon went spinning
through the air.
He bounced off the moon!
He made a terrible mess!
Dragon scales and 'O's everywhere!
He fell back down to earth.

Boo

And there he lay
in the middle, feeling
very sorry for himself.
   'I won't do it again,'
he sniffed.

   The Bookmouse
made the Snapdragon
return the 'O's to the
ghosts of the
Woollywolves in
the Moonwood.

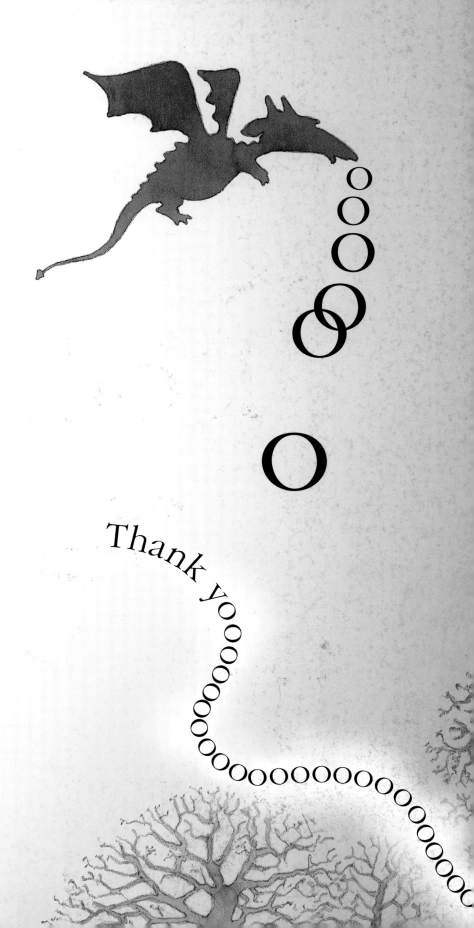

Thank yooooooooooooooooooooooooooo

And because he was really sorry, and not just pretending, the Snapdragon brought back the K he had stolen and put it back where it belonged...

Boo

k

...right at the end of the Book

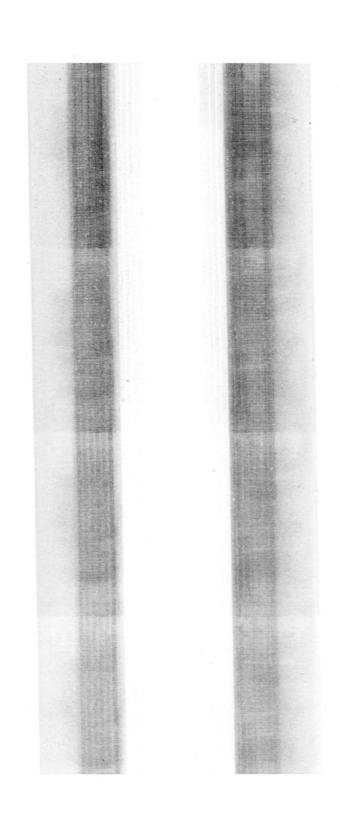